THE PUZZLE PLACE

Dear Parents,

The easy-to-read books in this series are based on The Puzzle Place™, public television's highly praised new show for children that teaches not ABC's or 123's, but "human being" lessons!

In these books, your child will learn about getting along with children from all different backgrounds, about dealing with problems, and making decisions—even when the best thing to do is not always so clear.

Filled with humor, the stories are about situations which all kids face. And best of all, kids can read them all on their own, building a sense of independence and pride.

So come along to the place where it all happens. Come along to The Puzzle Place™....

ISBN 0-448-41288-8 (pb) A B C D E F G H I J

ISBN 0-448-41331-0 (GB) A B C D E F G H I J

The Puzzle Place is a co-production of Lancit Media Productions, Ltd., and KCET/Los Angeles. Major funding provided by the Corporation for Public Broadcasting and SCEcorp.

DON'T CRY, LEON

By Roberta Edwards

Illustrated by William Langley

Based on the teleplay,
"Big Boys Don't Cry,"
by Ellis Weiner, Susan Amerikaner,
Jennifer Bross, and Judy Rothman Rofe

GROSSET & DUNLAP · NEW YORK

Leon has a new Build-O set.

It has 300 pieces.

He can build a Mega Star Ship.

It looks mega cool.

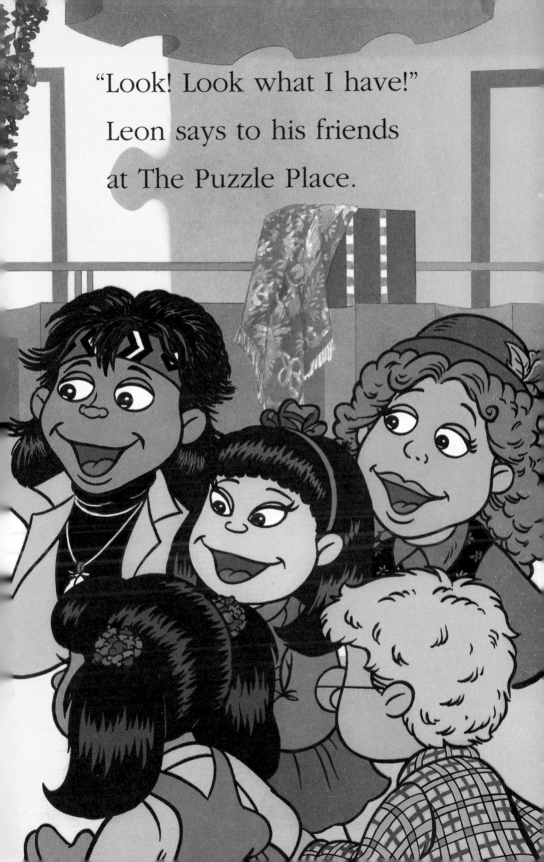

"Look! Look what I have!"
Leon says to his friends
at The Puzzle Place.

Right away
Ben takes the box
from Leon.
"Oh cool!" he says.
"I love Build-O sets."

The kids all open the box.
"We can build a bridge,"
Julie says.
"Or a tower," says Skye.

Leon says, "No. No.
I am going to show you
how to build
the Mega Star Ship.
You need all 300 pieces
to make it."

But nobody hears Leon.
Then Leon sees Ben
rip open a bag of pieces.
Pieces go flying all over.

What if a piece is lost?
Then Leon cannot make
the Mega Star Ship!
"Stop it!" Leon shouts.
"This is my Build-O set.
And you are all wrecking it!"

Now everybody looks up

at Leon.

Oh no!

Leon is crying.

Ben says, "Sorry, Leon."
But he does not sound
very sorry.
"Still, you don't have to be
such a crybaby!
Crying is for girls —
and babies!"

That does it!

Leon runs out of

The Puzzle Place.

Some friends they are!

"Well, he <u>was</u> a crybaby,"
Ben says to everybody.

"No, he wasn't," says Kiki.
"It was his new Build-O set.
We just grabbed it from him.
I don't blame Leon
for being mad."

Then Julie tells everybody
to find all the pieces.
She is going to find Leon.

Leon is in the playground.

He is just sitting

on a swing.

Julie puts on a funny pair
of nose glasses.
"Guess who?" she says to Leon.

Leon does not laugh.
So Julie takes off
the funny glasses.
"I just want to cheer you up.
We were not very nice."

Leon slides off the swing.

"Ben called me a crybaby."

Julie takes Leon's hand.
"Come back to
The Puzzle Place.
We will all make up."
But Leon shakes his head.
"I will get my Build-O set—
what's left of it.
Then I am going home."

Now Julie and Leon
are back at
The Puzzle Place.

"That's 299 pieces,"
Jody is saying.
She is putting them all
in the Build-O box.
"One is still missing."

Everybody looks hard.

Skye looks under the rug.

Kiki looks under the pillows.

Ben looks under a table.
They do not see that
Julie and Leon are back.

"I found it!" Ben shouts.

He gets up fast.

Uh-oh!

He forgets he is under a table.

Ouch!

Ben has hit his head—hard.

What do you know?

Ben is crying!

Ben rubs his head.
Then he wipes away
his tears.
He sees Leon,
and he goes over to him.

"I am sorry I called you
a crybaby," says Ben.
"I know boys cry.
Since my dad died,
sometimes I cry at night.
It is because I miss him."

Jody says,
"My dad's friend cried
when he lost his job."
Skye says,
"My father cried
when my little sister was born.
He was so happy."

Ben puts the lost piece
in the Build-O box.
He hands it to Leon.
"Are we friends again?"
asks Ben.
Leon smiles.
"Yes! And guess what
we can do now?"

Everybody shouts
at the same time,
"Build the Mega Star Ship!"